little

Cynthia Moss

❊

photographs by

Martyn Colbeck

❊

Simon & Schuster
Books for Young Readers

big ears

T H E   S T O R Y   O F   E L Y

SIMON & SCHUSTER BOOKS FOR YOUNG READERS

An imprint of Simon & Schuster Children's Publishing Division

1230 Avenue of the Americas, New York, New York 10020

Text copyright © 1997 by Cynthia Moss

Photographs copyright © 1997 by Martyn Colbeck

SIMON & SCHUSTER BOOKS FOR YOUNG READERS is a trademark of Simon & Schuster

Book design by Heather Wood / The text of this book is set in Cantoria

Printed and bound in the United States of America

10 9 8 7 6 5 4 3 2 1

Library of Congress Cataloging-in-Publication Data

Moss, Cynthia. Little big ears : the story of Ely / by Cynthia Moss

photographs by Martyn Colbeck. p. cm. Summary: Follows a young elephant

as he struggles to survive during his first year of life with the help of his family in

Amboseli, a protected wildlife park in Kenya. ISBN 0-689-80031-2 (hardcover)

1. African elephant—Kenya—Amboseli National Park—Biography—Juvenile

literature. 2. African elephant—Behavior—Kenya—Amboseli National Park—

Juvenile literature. 3. Amboseli National Park (Kenya)

[1. African elephant. 2. Elephants.] I. Colbeck, Martyn, ill. II. Title.

QL737.P98M675 1997 599.6'1—dc20 96-7404

To the children of Africa,
who hold the future of Africa's elephants in their hands

C. M. & M. C.

There is no winter in Africa. Here it is hot all the time. But right in the middle of Africa is a huge mountain called Kilimanjaro, which is so high that its peaks are covered with snow all year long.

At the bottom of Kilimanjaro is a wildlife park called Amboseli. Here it is warm and there are plenty of grasses and rich green swamps. Amboseli is home to many animals, including lions, leopards, cheetahs, buffaloes, giraffes, zebras, wildebeests, and gazelles. But it is perhaps best known for its elephants.

While many elephants in Africa are hunted and killed for their ivory tusks, the over eight hundred elephants in Amboseli live in peace. In this wildlife park they are protected from poachers. They are the best known elephants in Africa because they have been studied by scientists for many years. This is the story of one elephant family who lives in Amboseli.

Elephants live in families, as we do, but their families are different from ours. An elephant family is made up of mothers and calves, and is led by the oldest female, usually a grandmother. The father, grandfather, uncles, and older brothers live separately and only meet with the family for special occasions.

One of the most beautiful and gentle of the grandmother elephants now living in Amboseli is Echo, who has lovely, curved tusks. The leader of her family, Echo has given birth to many calves, including three daughters, named Erin, Enid, and Eliot. She is also the mother of Ely, a very special male calf.

A female elephant gives birth to a new calf every four to five years. In February 1990, Echo was due to have a new calf. As the time drew near, Echo seemed tired all the time. She had been pregnant for over twenty-one months (the typical term for elephants is 21 1/2 months or 660 days). Instead of leading her family, she trailed behind as the group moved around the park in search of food and water. She frequently stopped to rest, and the other members of the family, who were very loyal to her, waited for her to catch up.

Toward the end of February, Echo and her family were only traveling a couple of miles each day. Echo was huge and walked very, very slowly. Finally, early in the morning of February 28, she gave birth to a very large male calf. This was Ely.

As soon as Ely was born he started to struggle, kicking his legs and lifting his head to break through the birth sac. Echo reached down and ripped through the sac with her tusks. Soon Ely was trying to stand up. He managed to get his hind legs under him, but his front legs would not straighten. Something was wrong.

A half hour later, Ely got partway up on the first joints of his front legs. By straightening out his back legs he could kneel, but he was unsteady and kept falling down.

Elephants are very intelligent animals, and Ely's mother, Echo, and his older sister, Enid, could see right away that Ely had a problem. They kept urging him to stand by curling their trunks under his stomach and lifting him, while gently prodding him with the toes of their feet. But it was no use: the first joints of Ely's front legs were bent back and completely stiff.

An elephant calf can usually walk when it is less than an hour old, but after two hours Ely still could not walk. By this time the rest of the family had left to find food and water. Only Echo and Enid remained behind with Ely.

Ely must have been thirsty, but in order to drink his mother's milk he had to be able to reach her breast. To make matters worse, the hot African sun was beating down on them. Although there was shade nearby, Echo and Enid would not leave Ely. They continued to encourage him until eventually he began to take a few shuffling steps on his knees.

After two hours of very slow progress, the elephants moved a short distance to a small pool. Echo splashed some cooling mud on herself and Ely, which seemed to revive the baby elephant. He then made a huge effort to stretch up to Echo's breast. After several failures he finally reached the nipple. For the first time he drank the life-giving milk.

By the end of his first day of life, the chances for Ely's survival looked very bad. He would not starve to death, but he could not survive by shuffling around on his crippled legs. The skin would be rubbed raw and he would die of infection.

The next morning, though, Ely was stronger. He found that he could hobble along behind or next to his mother and sister, as long as they went very slowly and waited for him. Partway through the morning the rest of the family joined them. There was a great deal of rumbling, screaming, bellowing, and trumpeting as the elephants greeted one another. Ely was confused by all the excitement, but at the same time it was reassuring to have so many giant legs surrounding him and so many trunks reaching down to touch him.

Later on in the day something unexpected happened. Ely began to move his left front foot. Each time Echo stopped, Ely straightened his leg little by little. By the afternoon there was a definite change in Ely, and it looked as though his chances were improving.

That night the whole family fed and then slept near the palm trees. The next morning at dawn the elephants were still asleep—all except Ely, who was hard at work. He could now partially unbend both his front legs, and he continually stretched them against the ground or a log.

When he wasn't stretching he was trying to
stand. To do this, Ely started by leaning his body
backwards until his two front legs were almost
straight. Then, carefully and ever so slowly, he
leaned forward onto the soles of his front feet and
tried to straighten his legs, which were still too
weak to hold him. Down he went onto his knees
again. But Ely was fighting for his life and he
wouldn't give up. Finally, after many, many falls, he
made one last try. He got the soles of his front feet
firmly on the ground, leaned back, then forward,
rose up, and stayed up. It was only when he tried
to take a step forward that he crashed in a heap.
The important thing, though, was that he could
stand. With more practice and hard work he
would learn how to walk, too.

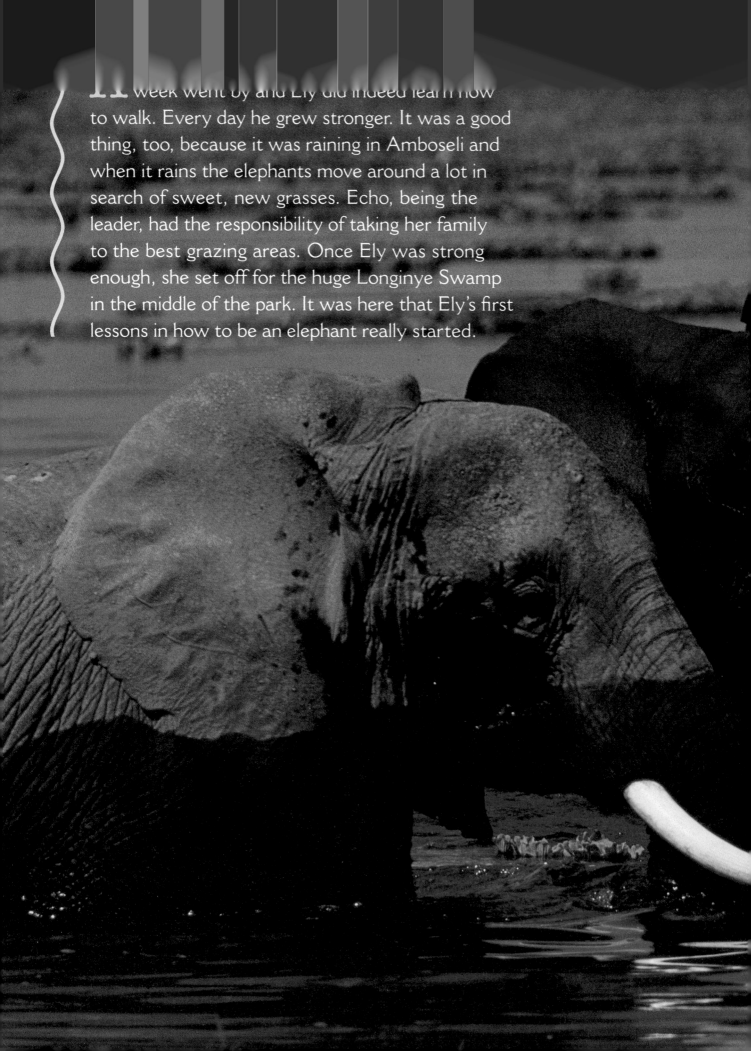

A week went by and Ely did indeed learn how
to walk. Every day he grew stronger. It was a good
thing, too, because it was raining in Amboseli and
when it rains the elephants move around a lot in
search of sweet, new grasses. Echo, being the
leader, had the responsibility of taking her family
to the best grazing areas. Once Ely was strong
enough, she set off for the huge Longinye Swamp
in the middle of the park. It was here that Ely's first
lessons in how to be an elephant really started.

He had much to learn. Echo walked up to the edge of the deep, muddy swamp and plunged right into the water. Ely seemed unsure what to do, but his sister Enid came up behind him and gently pushed him in. It was cold, yet at the same time there was something very nice about the squishy mud. Walking in it was a different matter. Keeping up with his mother was hard work, but he did it, and soon he found himself swimming beside her. It didn't take him long to discover that if he kept the tip of his trunk up out of the water he could breathe. Elephants have their own built-in snorkels.

As the days went by, Ely became better at walking, climbing, and swimming, but he had trouble using his trunk. An elephant's trunk is a very long nose, and it also works like our arm and hand. It can do all sorts of things, but it takes a lot of practice. At first Ely's trunk looked like a small, floppy rubber hose hanging off the end of his face. He didn't seem to know what to do with it, and it kept getting in his way. In fact, one day when he was walking along, he stepped on it, which hurt!

But soon he began to use it. When the family stopped to feed, he tried smelling and feeling things with his trunk. He used its two finger-like ends to hold onto sticks. If he wrapped his trunk around the stick properly, he could sometimes lift it in the air and wave it around, which he enjoyed. If there were no sticks to be found, he wrapped his trunk around Enid's tusk and pulled.

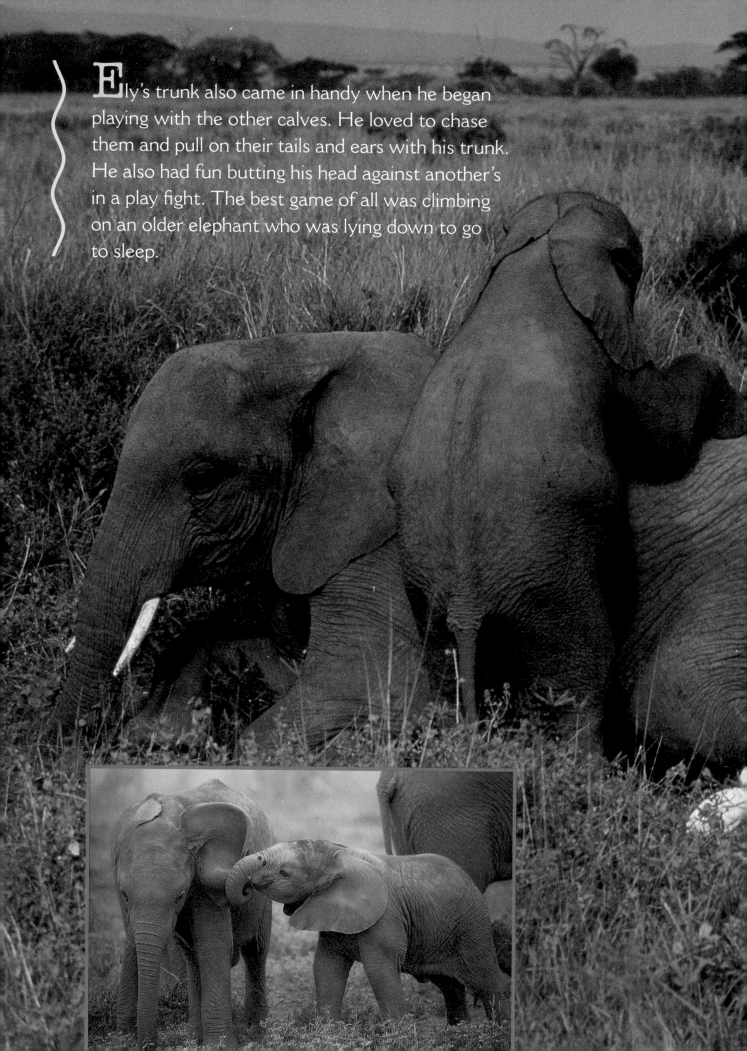

Ely's trunk also came in handy when he began playing with the other calves. He loved to chase them and pull on their tails and ears with his trunk. He also had fun butting his head against another's in a play fight. The best game of all was climbing on an older elephant who was lying down to go to sleep.

Ely was also learning how to feed himself. By the time he was three and a half months old he weighed nearly 350 pounds, and Echo's milk was no longer enough to satisfy him. He had to start eating grass and drinking water, but to do so wasn't easy at all.

An elephant eats grass by wrapping its trunk around a clump of it, ripping it from the roots, then lifting the clump to its mouth. In the beginning, Ely stole small amounts of food from his mother or sisters to learn what was good. He simply reached up to their mouths and pulled out some of what they were eating. Soon after that, he began to pull up one blade of grass at a time and tried to get it into his mouth. Sometimes he forgot what he was supposed to be doing, and when he finally got the grass in his trunk he would end up putting it on top of his head!

Learning how to drink was even more difficult. An elephant sucks water up into its trunk, lifts its head, puts its trunk in its mouth, and lets the water run down its throat. This is a very tricky maneuver for a young elephant. Most calves don't even try to do this until they are about six months old, but Ely was very determined to succeed. He started trying when he was four months old. Standing next to his cousins, he would dip his trunk in the water the same way they did, but then when he tried to suck up the water it went too high, which made him sneeze and blow all the water back out. It was going to take a lot more practice.

After a few more months and a great deal of patience, Ely finally managed to get some water into his mouth. One day, in his eagerness to practice his drinking skills, he got into trouble. He went off with his cousins, Elspeth and Esau, and Elspeth's mother to have a drink at a small pool that was covered in water lilies.

Just as he was about to dip his trunk in the water, a huge hippo burst out of the lilies and lunged straight at him. Ely turned and ran, bumping straight into Elspeth. Fortunately, the angry hippo trotted off in the other direction. This incident taught Ely to be a little more cautious when approaching a water hole. He still had much to learn if he was going to survive his first year.

Over the next months Ely got better and better
at feeding and drinking, and when he remembered,
he was a bit more careful about things like angry
hippos. But when Ely was nine months old, something happened in Amboseli that threatened his life.
There was a drought.

A drought happens when not enough rain falls
and the plants and grasses die. During the year that

Ely was born almost no rain fell at all in November and December. Soon all the grass turned brown and died, leaving nothing but dust.

It is in times like this that the grandmother-leader of the family is so important to elephants. Ely's mother, Echo, would have to get her family through the drought by finding food. But it was also up to Ely to eat enough of this food himself, and that was not going to be easy.

Once the grasses and other plants were gone, Echo led her family to the swamps every day to feed. Here there were reeds, sedges, water lettuces, lilies, and many other kinds of vegetation. At first Ely found enough food each day, but as the drought went on, most of the vegetation that he could chew was soon eaten up. In the evenings the elephants looked for food on dry ground, but even here Ely had problems, since he was too small to break the branches of trees and bushes, or to pull up roots.

Ely and the other calves soon discovered a peculiar way to get food: they ate the dung of the adults. It was a very sensible arrangement. The adults could chew the tough food, but they didn't digest everything they swallowed, and a lot of unused vegetation came back out in a nice, soft form. So, when an adult had eaten a particularly nutritious meal and later that day dropped it out in her dung, the little calves raced over and gobbled it up.

Two months passed and still there was no rain. Ely was eleven months old. He was still getting milk from Echo, but it was not enough to nourish him. His backbone and ribs had begun to show through his skin. Life was no longer fun. The family spent all its time searching for food or resting.

Finally, when Ely was just over a year old, thunder rumbled across the plains and cool, life-saving rain fell. Within a few days little green sprouts of grass came up. More rain fell and the grass grew and grew, and soon there was more than enough food. The rain also created rivers and ponds, and best of all, mudwallows. In a kind of elephant celebration, Echo took her family to one of the best wallows in the park. The mud was just the right consistency—like a huge tub of chocolate syrup. The whole family got in and completely covered themselves. The adults lay in the gooey mud, kicking from time to time. Ely and the other calves got very excited and splashed with their feet and trunks. They pushed and shoved each other, and got out on the bank and slid back down into the wallow, with a giant, plopping sound. This was the fun of being an elephant calf.

The drought was forgotten. Ely had made it
through his first year. Ahead were many challenges,
but he was now strong enough to face them.

EPILOGUE

Almost five years have passed since Ely celebrated his first birthday. He now stands over five feet tall at the shoulder and weighs nearly two thousand pounds. His tusks are close to eight inches long. When he was four years old, Ely was weaned from his mother, and since then he has been getting all his nourishment from grass and other plants. Right after Ely turned four, Echo gave birth to a new calf, his little sister, Ebony. Ely doesn't mind having a baby sister because he still gets a lot of attention from his mother. But Ebony's too small to be his playmate. Instead, Ely enjoys sparring with other male calves his own age. He is learning the skills he will need to become a strong adult male.

Cynthia Moss and Martyn Colbeck have completed two films about the life of Echo's family. The first film is called "Echo of the Elephants," and follows Ely's progress from birth to the age of fifteen months. The more recent film is "Echo of the Elephants: The Next Generation," which follows the family through four more years and features the birth of Ely's sister, Ebony.

The Amboseli elephants have been lucky so far. Most of Africa's elephants are rapidly losing the land they have lived on for thousands of years. And poachers who hunt them for their ivory tusks are an ever-present danger. If you'd like to help Ely and the other elephants remain safe, please send a donation to, or request further information from:

Amboseli Elephant Research Project
African Wildlife Foundation
1717 Massachusetts Avenue NW
Washington, D.C. 20036